Fox & Crow
A Christmas Tale

Zetta Elliott

Fox & Crow
A Christmas Tale

Illustrated by Babs Webb

Rosetta
Press

Books by Zetta Elliott

A Wish After Midnight
An Angel for Mariqua
Bird
Max Loves Muñecas!
Room in My Heart
Ship of Souls
The Boy in the Bubble
The Deep
The Girl Who Swallowed the Sun
The Last Bunny in Brooklyn
The Phoenix on Barkley Street

Fox woke at dusk and felt a rumble in his hollow belly. He shook off the snow that had settled on his fur and stretched his legs.

"Time to eat," he said to himself.

The field mice were busy beneath the deep snow. Fox heard them scurrying back and forth along their invisible tunnels. He took short, silent steps and then waited…and listened…and waited… and then Fox pounced!

Again and again Fox dove deep into the cold snow, but each time he surfaced without a tasty mouse between his sharp teeth.

From across the field, Crow watched as her old friend hunted unsuccessfully for mice. She had just devoured a moldy sardine from the trash bag Raccoon harvested from town. Humans were wasteful. The food they threw away could provide a small feast for hungry animals.

Finally Fox gave up and trotted over to the woods that separated the field from the town.

"You're slow today," said Crow from her perch on a tree stump.

"I'm hungry," Fox whined as he surveyed the contents of the torn trash bag. "I suppose you and Raccoon have picked every can clean."

"Look closer," Crow slyly suggested. "Perhaps you will find a tasty treat, too."

"I don't know where to begin," Fox said.

Mischief flashed in Crow's black eyes. Fox had played a trick on her last week and Crow saw a chance for revenge.

"Why not try that jar over there? Something sweet is stuck at the very bottom, I think, but I couldn't reach it with my short beak."

On any other day, Fox would not have been so quick to trust Crow. Today, however, Fox was too hungry to be wary. He sniffed inside the jar.

"It doesn't smell like fruit," Fox said.

"Really?" replied Crow quite innocently. "I was sure there was a peach inside."

Fox loved sugary things but humans rarely threw away the sweet treats he liked best. The jar was half-buried in the snow but it did look like something was stuck at the bottom. Fox poked his muzzle in and tried to get a better look. Suddenly he felt someone butt him from behind. Fox lost his footing and plunged headfirst into the snowbank.

"Hey—watch out!" Fox cried, but his voice didn't sound as loud as it should. Fox pulled his head out of the snowbank and tumbled backward onto the ground. A vinegary pickle fell into his eye. Fox tried to swat it away with his paw but he couldn't reach the pickle somehow. Fox tried again and heard his claws scratch against something cold, hard, and clear as ice. The glass jar was stuck on his head!

"CROW!" Fox roared. He lunged at the silly bird, but Crow easily flew out of reach.

"You've gotten yourself into a pretty pickle this time, haven't you?" taunted Crow.

Fox tugged at the jar with his front paws and then his back paws, but it would not budge. He stumbled around, knocking into tree trunks and stumbling over the garbage strewn across the snow.

Fox was so enraged by the sound of Crow's cackling that he swung about wildly and finally succeeded in knocking Crow off her feet. She landed on the lid of the pickle jar and WHOOSH! Crow went skidding across the snow!

Suddenly Crow had an idea. Sometimes she watched humans

sledding down the big hill on the other side of town. They weren't very fast on their own two feet but when humans sat on their plastic discs, they whizzed down the hill like the wind.

"Alright, Crow, you've had your fun. Now help me!" pleaded Fox in desperation.

But Crow flew away with the lid in her beak and left Fox on his own.

Crow didn't head for the big hill. The sun hadn't yet set and that meant humans, big and small, would still be out sledding. Crow searched instead for her own private slope, and she found just what she was looking for in a quiet neighborhood. The steep roofs of the houses were covered with snow—a perfect place to try out her new sled!

Crow landed on the chimney of a house that was covered with gaudy flashing lights. Worried she might get tangled in all the wires, Crow took her makeshift sled over to the house next door. Crow didn't understand Christmas, but she knew that some humans cut down pine trees and brought them into their homes for a little while. Crow could see one such tree through the window of the house next door. It, too, was covered in lights, and colorful balls dangled from every branch. Boxes tied with ribbon were stacked on the floor all around the tree.

Crow was so busy studying the Christmas tree that she almost didn't see the human lying in a bed nearby. A sullen little boy was propped up with pillows, and he looked quite miserable despite all the flashing lights and shiny ornaments on the tree. There was a tray loaded with food on a bedside table, but it looked like the boy hadn't eaten a single bite. Crow knew all that food would wind up in the garbage, and so she decided to tell Raccoon to pay a visit to this house later on.

"Humans are so wasteful!" Crow muttered disdainfully before turning her attention back to her sled.

Crow set the lid down on the snow at the very top of the roof. Then she hopped onto it and waited to go flying down the slope. But the lid only sank into the deep snow. Crow bent down and pecked at the lid, hoping to prod it forward with her beak, but the lid just sank deeper and refused to go.

Crow thought for a moment. She glanced about and noticed that the snow was not as thick on other parts of the roof. Crow picked up the lid with her beak and flew to a spot with only a thin layer of snow. She set the lid down, hopped onto it, and WHOOSH! Crow zoomed down the roof!

The lid slowed as it neared the roof's edge and dropped into the eaves. Crow plucked it out with her beak and flew back to the top of the roof. Over and over Crow slid down the rooftop, sending up whorls of snow that glittered in the icy air.

A sudden movement at the window next door caught Crow's eye. She hopped to the edge of the roof and saw that the ugly little boy was no longer in bed. His face was pressed against the frosty windowpane, and his wide eyes were fixed on Crow.

Crow returned to the rooftop and skidded back down with as much poise as she could muster. She glanced over at the window and saw that the boy was clapping! Crow took up the lid and gave

a repeat performance.

"Bravo! Bravo!"

Crow didn't know just what that word meant, but she could tell that the boy was admiring her. Moonlight gave her glossy, black feathers a violet tint that was quite lovely to behold. Crow preened a bit before flying up to the rooftop with the lid clamped in her beak.

"Watch this," said Crow. She balanced on the lid and then used her wingtip to twirl the disc as it went skidding down the snowy roof. Crow felt a bit dizzy when she reached the roof's edge. She looked over at the boy and saw that his face was glowing with delight. His eyes shone brighter than the flashing lights strung along the roof.

"He looks quite nice when he smiles," thought Crow. She picked up the lid and flew back up to the rooftop, anxious to impress him once more.

Just then a woman came into the room and pulled the boy away from the window. Crow set the lid down and watched as the boy reluctantly followed his mother's orders and climbed back into bed. He pointed at the window as if to tell his mother about Crow's cleverness, but she only frowned before yanking the curtains shut.

"Well!" said Crow. "How rude."

She hopped onto the lid and slid down the roof once more but it wasn't as thrilling without an audience.

Crow felt rather alone on the moonlit roof. She felt a sudden desire to tell Fox about the little boy, but he wouldn't want to listen while that jar was stuck on his head. Crow wondered if Fox had managed to get it off yet, and wished she hadn't played such a silly trick on him. Crow clamped the lid tightly in her beak and flew off to look for her old friend.

But Fox wasn't waiting for Crow to return. He had decided to solve the problem on his own.

First, Fox ate the horrid pickle so that it no longer fell in his eye. Then Fox set out in search of someone who could help him remove the jar from his head. Shadows grew as the sun sank in the sky and Fox's breath fogged up the glass, making the familiar forest look scary and strange. Raccoon would be able to pull the jar off his head, but Raccoon was nowhere to be found. No doubt she was already in town, scavenging for food.

Fox tried to shatter the glass jar by knocking his head against trees and rocks. But the sturdy jar remained unbroken and Fox

only succeeded in giving himself a terrible headache. Finally Fox stumbled clumsily through the woods and got as close to town as he dared. His head hung low for the jar was as heavy as his shame.

Normally Fox did his best to avoid humans. Hunters with guns chased his kind through the forest, and even small humans took aim with their slingshots and stones. Fox knew it was risky being this close to town, but he didn't know what else to do. He would have to ask a human for help.

When he reached the edge of the woods, Fox propped his head up on a rock so that he could see people coming and going. Across the busy road there was a row of shops. Their windows were filled with bright lights, and a bell jingled every time someone opened or closed a shop door. A man playing carols on an accordion was standing at one end of the street. A little girl stood beside him holding an empty tin can.

Fox scanned the street for someone with empty hands and a kind face. He spotted a man peering into one of the shop windows. The little girl wandered over to the man but she didn't beg for coins. Instead she gazed longingly at the toys on the other side of the glass. The man noticed her and dropped a handful of change into her can. The girl thanked him, pulled herself away from the toy store, and went back to the man with the accordion.

Fox knew he had to hurry. Once night fell, the stores would close and the humans would disappear inside their homes. Fox took a deep breath and dashed across the street—and was nearly hit by a car! The screeching brakes and loud horn blast made the man turn away from the toy store window. He peered into the gathering darkness and saw a trembling fox creeping toward him—with a jar

on its head!

"What have we here?" asked the man.

"Be careful," warned the man with the accordion. "A fox like that could have rabies!"

The coins in the tin can rattled as the little girl hurried to hide behind her father's legs.

Fox froze in his tracks. The humans looked frightened. Would they go and get a gun? Fox felt his heart beating fast and feared he had made a terrible mistake.

But the man by the toy store wasn't afraid. He squatted down and held out his hand to Fox. "Come here, little fellow," said the man. "I won't hurt you."

Fox heard kindness in the man's voice and so took a few steps forward. The man reached out and took hold of the jar. Fox pulled back with all his strength but his head was still stuck.

The man eased forward and placed his other hand on Fox's neck.

"Oh, no!" thought Fox. "He's going to strangle me!"

But the man's fingers were surprisingly gentle. "Easy now," he said in a soothing voice. "We're almost there."

Fox forced himself to stand still and after a few uncomfortable moments, the man was able to pull the jar off his head.

"I'm free!" cried Fox. His amber eyes burned bright as he did a little dance of joy.

The girl had never seen a fox dance before and let out a startled scream. She dropped her can and the coins scattered silently upon the snowy ground.

Fox stopped dancing. He realized he'd better head back into

the woods where he belonged. But first Fox looked up at the man who had freed him and thanked him for his help. He knew that humans couldn't understand Fox tongue, but he was so grateful that he thanked the man again.

"Wait until my son hears about this!" said the man with a smile.

"It's a tale better than any toy."

Then he reached into his pocket, took out some bills, and folded them into the little girl's tin can. The man put his hands in his pockets and walked away.

Fox scanned for the bright headlights of oncoming cars before dashing back across the road and disappearing into the night.

When Crow reached the clearing in the woods, Fox was sitting alone in the snow, staring up at the sky. The silly pickle jar was nowhere to be seen.

Crow coughed nervously to get Fox's attention. "I've had quite a remarkable evening," she said.

"So have I," answered Fox.

Crow couldn't detect any anger in Fox's voice. In fact, she had never seen Fox look so serene. Crow wanted to tell him all about her adventure in town. She also wanted to ask how he'd gotten the jar off his head, but Crow felt she ought to apologize first. Crow opened her beak to suggest a truce, but no sound came out.

For a long while Fox and Crow sat in silence with the bright star sparkling high above them like a diamond.

"Humans can surprise you," Crow said quietly.

"Indeed, they can," Fox replied before trotting off to hunt for his supper.

THE END

About the Author

Zetta Elliott is the award-winning author of twelve books for young readers. She lives in Brooklyn and loves birds, foxes, and the magic of Christmas.

Learn more at zettaelliott.com

About the Illustrator

Babs Webb is a Mexican-American illustrator with a BFA from Pratt Institute. Working predominantly in graphite, she enjoys capturing a classical style reminiscent of old etchings and reliefs. Webb currently resides in the mountains of Colorado with her partner and the overweight cat they both generously feed.

Learn more at babswebb.carbonmade.com

37185752R00021

Made in the USA
Charleston, SC
27 December 2014